# THORNHILL

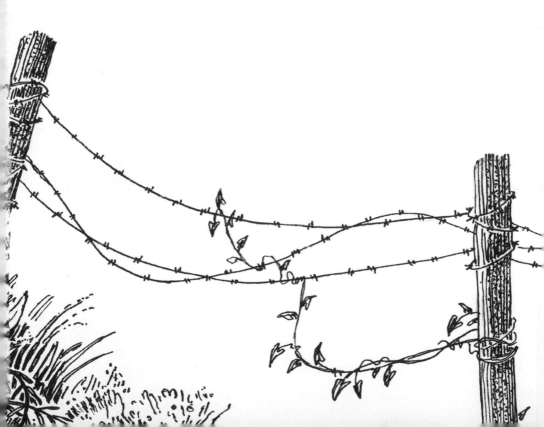

# THORNHILL

Pam Smy

ROARING BROOK PRESS
NEW YORK

Text and illustrations copyright © 2017 by Pam Smy.
Published by Roaring Brook Press
Roaring Brook Press is a division of Holtzbrinck Publishing Holdings Limited Partnership
175 Fifth Avenue, New York, NY 10010
mackids.com

Library of Congress Cataloging in Publication Control Number: 2017001991 (print)

Our books may be purchased in bulk for promotional, educational,
or business use. Please contact your local bookseller or the
Macmillan Corporate and Premium Sales Department
at (800) 221-7945 ext. 5442 or by e-mail at
MacmillanSpecialMarkets@macmillan.com.

First published in Great Britain in 2017 by David Fickling Books

First American edition 2017
Printed in China by RR Donnelley Asia Printing
Solutions Ltd., Dongguan City, Guangdong Province

10 9 8 7 6 5 4 3 2 1

For my husband

February 8, 1982

I knew it was too good to last. She is back. Without even looking I knew it. I heard her laughter echoing up the stairwell, the usual thumping on each of the doors in the corridor as she made her way back to her old room. I froze as I heard those sounds. Fear tingled into my neck and down my back as the old feeling seeped into my bones.

I don't believe it.

What will I do now?

I've decided to lock myself away. Now that she is back it is the only way I can keep myself safe. I'll tell them I am ill or something. They'll probably not even notice I'm not down there anyway. As long as I don't have to see her. As long as I don't have to face her, look her in the eye, hear her voice. Yes, locking myself away is the answer.

It's great up here, actually. I am the only girl with my own sink and bathroom. I love having the highest room in the whole building, being able to look up at the topmost branches of the trees outside. I can watch the birds skim past, fast and free. Carefree.

And from up here I overlook the houses where the real people, the regular people, live. Sometimes I watch them sleepily opening their curtains in the mornings, heaving out their garbage bags in their bathrobes, letting out their cats, feeding the birds. In the summer they have friends round and there's noisy laughter and tinkling glasses in the gardens, and on hot days I watch the squealing children splashing in wading pools or squabbling over tricycles. You know, regular, real people with regular, real families. Of course, sometimes that is all a bit much and I have to shut them out too.

Yes, it's not bad up here. Locking myself away won't be hard at all.

# February 14, 1982

I started to make another figure today. I have molded the body, arms, and legs. I am making it small, like a child. Not sure who it will be yet.

So far, I seem to be getting away with staying up here. I am going down when I know the others are all in front of the TV and Kathleen is bustling around in her apron, clearing up the dining hall. She knows. She knows I am not coming down to eat with the others and that I'm bringing down yesterday's tray and restacking it with bread rolls, packets of biscuits, yogurts, and apples. She watches me, gives me a wink, and lets me get on with it. I like Kathleen. She's nice.

Even stealing downstairs for those five minutes each day makes me sick with fear. My palms prickle with slippery sweat, my heart pounds in my ears, and even when I am safely back up here it takes a while for my hands to stop shaking.

It is a feeling I haven't had for months. When she left to be fostered last time, I could breathe again. I felt as though I had been holding my breath for years. The other girls weren't exactly friendly after she left, but it's just that they left me alone. They don't speak to me because they don't get a reply, so mostly they act as though I am not there. Invisible. That can feel lonely, but I am used to that. Loneliness is nothing compared to the crush of fear I have when *she* is here at Thornhill.

I can understand their adoration of her. If you were to describe us the first words would be the same. Both blond, blue-eyed girls of thirteen. But my hair is long and limp. Hers bounces in natural ringlets. My eyes are small with dark shadows under them. Hers are big and round and pretty. I'm always frowning. She looks like a rosy-cheeked doll. The others follow her like puppies, desperate to catch some of her beauty, impress her so that she rewards them with one of those beautiful smiles.

Luckily for me, though, I haven't seen her yet—I think she is leaving me alone. Sometimes I hear her walking along the hallway below, the familiar stomp and howls of laughter if she is with her old friends or, if she is on her own, the thump, thump, thump on each of the doors she passes. I shake then too. Sometimes I wake up in the night, that noise filling my head. That thump, thump, thump fills me with terror—even in my dreams. Thump, thump, thump. I lie there cold with fear and remembering.

Thump.


Thump.


Thump.

## February 16, 1982

Getting a bit fed up with bread rolls and yogurt.

## February 17, 1982

I started rereading *The Secret Garden* today. I read it years ago, but I had forgotten loads of it. The girl in it is called Mary too and her parents die right at the beginning of the story, so she is on her own, like me. But she can speak whenever she chooses, so I guess she isn't like me. She is supposed to be the heroine, but for a main character she isn't very likable. Sickly looking. Yellow, pasty skin. Sharp features. Always cross with people. I rather like it that she isn't one of the usual type—those pretty ones who are always kind and patient despite the terrible hardships they face. Life just isn't like that. Mine isn't anyway.

This Mary is picked on by the other kids too. They chant a nursery rhyme, *"Mary, Mary, quite contrary,"* at her and she just ignores it. To be fair, even I could probably ignore a bit of name-calling.

I have decided to make my new figure into Mistress Mary Quite Contrary. Right after school I curled up on the floor under the window and worked away at the clay, pinching and sliding it around until a head began to appear. It was quite tricky to shape the face as I imagined it—sharp pointy nose and chin, sunken little eyes. I enjoyed it, though. It is strange how the evening slips by when you are absorbed in something.

I often wonder what my life would be like without my puppets. I think about the other girls who don't have a passion for making or imagining and wonder what they do with their time. I wonder if they are bored. I am never bored. I am learning all the time, not just about different types of puppets from around the world or in history, but about the making of small bodies and figures and clothes and hair and eyes and shoes. And I love that I am surrounded by the things I have made. They sit on shelves above my bed, on my bookcase, suspended from the ceiling, balanced on my windowsill—my puppets are like friends that sit and keep me company. They watch me as I make their companions or add new ideas and designs to my sketchbook. I think that some people would find it creepy having all these little eyes watching them—but I don't. When I go into the dining hall and see all those old photos of the unnamed girls who have lived here over the last hundred years, all lined up in ghostly groups—that's scary. But my dolls are my comfort. In some way, even though I am often on my own, with my puppets about me, I don't feel so alone.

February 25, 1982

My luck has run out.

Jane came up to my room today. Of course it would be Jane. Of all the caregivers she is the one who actually seems to care. She has a lovely smile and a nice way about her. Sometimes she pats the back of my hand and at Christmas she gives me a hug. I can actually speak to Jane if I am up here in the safety of my room. I don't know what it is about Pete and Sharon, but my voice gets stuck and I can't reply to them, even in a whisper, even up here. But with Jane it is easier. She is the one who would have noticed something was wrong. I heard her soft steps before the gentle tap at the door.

"Hello," she said. "Can I come in?"

Before I tried to answer she was in already, easing herself onto the bed with a smile as if she was my best buddy. Sometimes I have to remind myself that she is paid to do this. It's her job. I just sat and waited to hear what she had to say.

"Wow! Look at these new puppets! They're really fab, Mary! There are quite a few new ones since I was up here last."

I didn't say anything.

She picked up Mistress Mary. "Oh! Is this one you? It looks just like you, you clever thing!"
I didn't say anything.

I hoped she wasn't going to keep up this cheerful, chattery stuff. It didn't sound right up here. She chatted a bit about Princess Di expecting a baby and about Thornhill closing and about where the other girls would be going. Then it went a bit quiet and she said:
"I just thought I'd pop up 'cause I hadn't seen you for a while and I wanted to know how you were. How are you?"
I just looked at her wide face and smiley pink-lipsticked mouth. She was fiddling nervously with Mistress Mary. Mary's head was lolling from side to side as Jane turned her over and over.
"Ahem . . . Well . . . I thought I hadn't seen you and I asked around and thought that maybe you were avoiding coming down because . . . well . . . because a certain person is back."
I went cold. Blink. Look natural, I thought. Say nothing. I blinked again.

"Since she came back I've noticed that you aren't spending time with us. You leave for school really early in the morning. I know you were never keen on being with us in the TV room, but I haven't even seen you in the dining hall. I'm not even sure you're eating properly. *Are you eating, Mary?*"

I stared at her. This was too much. Too close. I didn't want it talked about. I didn't want to listen. I tried to block out the words and just focus on Jane's hands as she tipped Mistress Mary over and over. I tried not to hear, but I couldn't help it. As she chatted away I heard phrases like, "we have to pity her," "difficult to be rehomed," "you must remember what it is like to be sent back here after thinking you have been placed with a family," "she must feel rejected," and "you should give her a chance to be friends."

That's when I snapped out of it.

Friends?

Friends!

"*Would* you, Mary? If I have a word with her and ask her to be friends, would you try too?"

Could she be serious? Did she know what she was suggesting?

"I know it is more difficult for you, Mary, with

56

your speaking issues and all, but . . . if you could?

"I am going to go down now and have a chat with her, Mary, and tomorrow you can come down and have breakfast with the rest of us. It'll be much better for everyone here at Thornhill if we can all get along. I'll come and knock for you in the morning so we can go down together. Okay, Mary?"

It sounded like a question but really it was an instruction.

I was aware that I was staring back. Blink. My eyes ached. Remember this so you can write it down later. Blink. My jaw ached. Remember what she is asking of you. Blink. I felt cold.

"Well, I am glad that is all sorted out," she said.

Jane stood up and walked out, clicking the door shut behind her. I like Jane, but she is really wrong this time.

I hadn't said a word.

I noticed that she had left Mistress Mary sprawled out on the bed, her arms and legs twisted under themselves. Mary's head was facedown on the pillow.

Maybe I imagined that everyone seemed to go quiet when Jane and I walked into the dining hall this morning. I felt completely stupid walking beside her as she chatted in the slightly overchirpy, overenthusiastic way of hers. Everyone must have known she had made me come down. I felt their eyes following us as we wove through the dining hall tables and up to Kathleen at the kitchen hatch. I kept my eyes down and didn't look at any of them. I knew my face was burning red, but I felt the usual cold fear all over. *She* was there in the room. I could feel her eyes on me. Kathleen gave me a smile and a wink as I loaded toast onto my plate with a shaking hand.

Jane began to talk to some of the other girls at another table, so I slid into a chair at an empty table and tried to look as though I was concentrating really hard on spreading the butter on my toast.

I knew who it would be when someone sat in the opposite chair.

"Hey, Mary," she said. "Great to see you."

She began to talk. It all sounded a little too loud, as if she wanted the others to hear too. She went on about how it was tough being sent back here and that she'd had to think about how she behaved and that she was turning over a new leaf and she wondered if I would think about forgiving her for everything that had happened and · could we be friends now?

Her speech was finished. The dining hall was silent. Everyone was listening, watching, waiting to see what I would do. I realized that the only sound was the rattling of my knife on my plate as my hand trembled. I put it down and hoped no one else had heard it.

Jane bustled over and broke the silence.

"Thank you, girls. It is great to think that we can all get along so well here," Jane said, and hurried out of the room.

Steadily *she* drew back the chair and stood up.

"I *really* mean it this time, Mary," she said as she followed Jane out of the room.

Table by table groups of girls went out too. I watched them go until I was the only one left in the dining hall. Just me and Kathleen, who had watched the whole performance through the hatch.

She shook her head and made a tutting sound.

"I know I shouldn't say it, but I wouldn't trust that one as far as I could throw her," she grumbled as I passed her plates from the empty tables. "She's all smiles and eyelashes and they follow her around like she's a princess, but those sweet smiles don't wash with me. There's a reason why she keeps being sent back here. Why no one will keep her . . . "

I must have had a look on my face because she hurriedly added, "I know you haven't been able to settle anywhere yet, Mary—but that's different. People find the quietness unsettling, that's all. One day there'll be someone special who doesn't expect you to be jabbering on all the time and you'll have a proper home, better than this creaking old place."

She ruffled my hair.

"You better be off to school. Here, take these." And she handed me a mini packet of ginger cookies.

As I left the dining hall she called out, "You look after yourself, Mary."

# March 1, 1982

Well, today *did* go better than I had hoped. They were all waiting outside the front door in a big huddle when Jane brought me down. *She* was there, I could sense it, but she didn't say anything and we all shifted off slowly toward school.

The hairs were up on the back of my neck the whole time we walked. My heart was pounding. But it was quite nice to have other people to walk to school with. They didn't chat much to me directly and I hung near the back of the group so I didn't have to be with *her,* but the others still walked with me and I listened to them chatting about their favorite bands, boys in class, and TV shows.

It was good not to be on my own all day.

A couple of them walked home with me too. I came straight up to my room when we got back and they all bundled noisily into the TV room. But that's okay. It isn't as bad as it could have been.

## March 2, 1982

This morning was much like yesterday. We all walked to
school in one noisy gang of Thornhill girls.

I am not sure what to make of it.

When she came back, I was convinced that she was
going to start up again, pick up from where she left off. I
was sure she was going to be my tormentor. But now that
I think back on it, except for being her usual, noisy self,
she hasn't been interested in me at all.

Could she actually have turned over a new leaf?

Could Jane have been right that we should try to
get along?

## March 8, 1982

Today she walked with me. The others just carried on chattering, but she slowed and walked at my pace. She asked me how I was. I didn't raise my head to answer, I just kept watching the ground. She carried on talking anyway, telling me what it had been like with the last foster family. At first I was tense and worried but found myself being more and more curious.

What it made me realize was that *she* wants to belong somewhere just as much as *I* do.

## March 11, 1982

I didn't spend the evening in my room tonight. I joined them in the TV room and watched *Top of the Pops*. Jane sat in at the back of the room. I sat near the back too, watching as they shouted at the screen as their favorite bands flashed up on the chart countdown. When they played the number-one single they all jumped up and danced around the room, singing along as the singer pranced about on the stage, wearing a string vest.

Jane and I sat and watched them all. She muttered something about this song being ages old and that her parents used to listen to it. Then she said the best night to join them was Saturday. They all loved watching *Dallas*. She wanted me to join them, and, as I watched the other girls yelping and leaping around the room and giggling with each other, I decided I would.

# March 13, 1982

It's late. I am writing this in bed, thinking about all the changes this week.

All the years I have been here I could never have imagined that I would have a week like this one. I feel part of things. Part of a normal life—well, as normal as life in a place like Thornhill can be.

Have things changed for me at last?

It's so different to walk to school as part of the group, to hear laughter and chatter around me. *Now* I understand what their jokes are about and why they are teasing each other, and knowing what's going on makes it sound less cruel and threatening. I like the noise of being surrounded by a group. It's as though there are little stories whizzing around—dreams of pop groups and boyfriends, gossip about eyeliner and shoes and teachers. I don't have to join in, but still I feel part of their gang—on the edges looking in, watching, listening, but happy to be included.

Even at school it makes a difference. I know what they are talking about because I have watched some of the same TV shows and on Monday they'll be chatting about *Dallas*, and I'll know who Sue Ellen is at last and why J. R. is so nasty.

I wonder if *they* have accepted me because *she* has? It's odd, because before she came back, the rest of them behaved as if I was invisible—as if being silent meant I didn't count. But now they include me in conversations and chat around me. Even *she* has talked to me a few times too.

I feel part of the group.

I remember how it was before, how frightened I used to be. I know what she *can* be like—or used to be like.

April 4. 1982

I can't believe what has happened.

I can't believe I have been so stupid.

She told me yesterday afternoon that they were going to meet after dark to have a moonlit picnic, to celebrate Sophie going to a new foster family next week, and that she wanted me to come along. She told me that the old days, when they would have considered going without me, were gone, and that I am one of them now.

I left my room at midnight and crept down to their landing. The wind outside was whistling through the chimney pots and made the whole adventure seem more dramatic. I was so excited. They were smiling and welcoming, grinning and winking at me as we tiptoed down the main staircase and past Jane's door.

It was only when we got to the dining hall door that I realized I hadn't even thought about where the food was coming from.

*She* was standing by the pantry door.

She put one arm around me and said, "This treat is

for us. Just you and me, Mary."

She unlocked the door and we went down the thin flight of steps into the cupboard–like room, lined with tins, packets, jars, and bottles. She pointed to a bottle on the top shelf, up by the tiny window.

"That's Kathleen's cooking sherry." She grinned. "Come on, give me a leg up!"

She hooked her foot into my interlocked hands and tried to heave herself up a couple of times, but she didn't even get close to the shelf.

"Hang on, Mary. I'll get a chair."

I stood there, waiting for her to come back. I noticed a thin trail of ants threading along the baseboard. I watched them almost absent–mindedly as I waited.

When she did return, the others followed. They gathered around the door as she brought the chair in.

"If we use the back of the chair to stand on we should be able to reach. You go, Mary. You're lighter than me. I'll hold the chair steady."

She gave me one of those beautiful smiles.

I stepped onto the seat of the chair and put one foot on the chair's back. It had gone quiet. Their eyes were all on me. A prickling unease crept over me.

"Go on, Mary. Climb up," she said as she held down the seat of the chair.

I reached out and held on to one of the highest shelves, then brought my other foot up onto the chair back. My hands were sweaty. I was shaking. I looked down over my shoulder at them all.

"God, you're an idiot!" she said.

And she let go of the chair.

I fell. Suddenly clattering to the ground. Swiping jars to the floor which smashed all around me as I landed in a heap.

There were howls of laughter. The chair was pulled out. They ran back up to the kitchen. The door slammed shut and the pantry light went off.

I lay there in the darkness as they shrieked with laughter.

I had banged my head and my cheek was bleeding. I tried to sit up and felt the sharp pricks of glass shards in my hands and heels. I couldn't see what I was sitting in but it was cold and sticky and there was a lot of it.

"You didn't *really* think *we* could be friends with *you*, did you?" she said through the door.

The other girls' voices drifted away.

I felt an ant crawl between my fingers.

Another over my ankle.

"You didn't *really* think *I* could be friends with *you*, did you? Just look at you. You're a mess!"

She knew it without seeing me.

She was right.

I was a disgusting mess.

"Look at you, Mary. Who would want you?"

The kitchen light went out and the thin sliver of light beneath the pantry door vanished, leaving just an eerie glimmer of moonlight from the high window above the top shelf.

And it began as I knew it would.

She began to thump on the door.

Thump.
Thump.

Thump.
Thump.

Thump.
Thump.

Thump.
Thump.

The noise filled my head.

Thump.
Thump.

Thump.
Thump.

The darkness swelled and vibrated around me.

Thump.
Thump.

Thump.
Thump.

Thump.
Thump.

And then the fear swallowed me into blackness.

Kathleen found me this morning.

I had jam in my hair.

A bruised and bloody cheek.

My hands and feet were cut from shards of glass and I was sitting in my pajamas in a pool of jam, honey, and my own pee.

She came right in and knelt there in that pool of mess and hugged me and stroked my sticky hair and told me it would be all right.

But I know it won't be.

*I* know that this is just the beginning.

Ella,
Sorry, love - had to go
into work early and I'll
be home late again too.
Can you sort yourself
out for dinner tonight?
See you tomorrow,
Love Dad

I have spent days and days in bed.

I can't face school.

I don't want to see anyone.

I can't even read.

I have just been sitting here, wrapped in a blanket, watching the clouds pass the window. My hands won't stop trembling. My mind runs over it all again and again. I am so stupid. I should have seen it coming.

I ache with the effort of not crying. I won't let her make me cry. Not ever. But I want to. I want to let tears roll down my cheeks as I tell someone how scared I was. I want to sob out my disappointment that really they were all just pretending to like me.

Instead I sit here in the quiet, watching the birds and the clouds.

The cuts on my hands and feet are healing. The outside signs that anything happened are disappearing.

But inside I am broken.

Of course, from that day onward, the night visits

started just as they had done before she left the last time.
    She waits until the quiet hours then creeps up here.

    While the rest of the house sleeps *she* stands and
scratches and scrapes and bangs at my door.

    Thump.
    Thump.
    Thump.

    The noise is terrifyingly loud to me in the darkness,
but protected from the rest of the house by the heavy fire
door at the bottom of my stairs.
    I barely sleep at night, and during the day I sit here
shaking, quaking, the sound of those thumps echoing in
my head.

## April 30, 1982

My life is a nightmare.

It has begun as I knew it would.

I have only been back at school a week but already they are making my life hell.

My days are full of taunts, tricks, and practical jokes.

My nights are haunted by her.

I am suspicious of everyone.

Jumpy.

On edge.

On the edge.

Today it was the old nudged-elbow trick. I had a tray loaded with steaming beef and cabbage and a glass of water when one of her minions shoved into me, knocking my arm and sending the tray clattering to the ground. I looked straight across the room to her in time to catch her nod of approval to the culprit, Julie, who was now making exaggerated apologetic noises as the others sniggered. I had gravy down my skirt and beef splattered on my shoes. The water had formed a puddle at my feet.

"Have you peed yourself again, Mary?" someone asked.

I helped Kathleen clear up the mess.

The problem is that *she* is being so careful not to be caught. She is never anywhere near when disaster strikes. But I know it's her.

I had PE earlier this week. She had switched the sneakers in my gym bag. The sneakers there weren't mine and they were way too small. I squeezed into them (the usual giggling sounds from the other side of the bench) and hobbled onto the hockey field. Then, right under Miss Greene's nose, they made sure I was the target, swiping at my ankles instead of the ball whenever I was involved in a tackle. They kept passing the ball to me—and straightaway another girl would be there, hacking at my legs with her hockey stick. At one point they actually knocked me down and a group of them gathered around—all fake concern and cooing noises. Miss Greene just blew her whistle and play resumed. The girls running off down the field, laughing, leaving me in a muddy heap on the field. It felt as if the game went on forever.

When I got back into the changing rooms, I waited

until they were out of the showers before I went in alone, the bruises already beginning to show on my legs. I stood under the warm spray, but then someone turned off the cold so that scalding hot water spurted over me. I know it was her. More sniggering as I rushed out, naked, to avoid being burned. My towel had fallen off the hook outside the showers and was sopping wet. At least when I got back into the changing room my own sneakers were there on the bench under my bag.

And that was just PE. It's been like that all week.

I don't know that *she* arranged for all the water jugs in the dining hall to have salt in them—and that everyone else knew except me.

I don't know how *she* got ahold of my history book to write "Mrs. Evans is a fat cow" all over my homework. I had two lunchtime detentions for that.

I don't know when *she* got into the art room to carefully slice the head and arms off my sculpture. It had been done cleanly with a knife—she hadn't even bothered to make it look like it had been accidentally knocked over.

Even today, as I came back up here to change, the door handle came off in my hand. How did she do that? It took Jane and Pete ages to fix it while I stood there like an idiot, gravy drying into a crispy brown sludge on my skirt. I know it's her, but I just can't prove it.

And, of course, I know as I write this from the safety of my room that tonight, when the whole house is asleep and silent, she'll be back up here and the scratching and scraping and rattling and banging on my door will start again. And I know I will lie here cowering and shaking.

In *The Secret Garden*, when Mistress Mary heard noises in the night, she was brave enough to explore that creepy old house. But I am not so brave. I can't just open the door and face her. I know that she will be on one side of the door and that I will be on this side and that, although there is a barrier between us, she has a way of making the fear creep into my bones and pulse in my head that is more terrifying than I can describe.

I can live with being tormented by her during the day, but the terror I feel at night is unbearable.

## May 1, 1982

A few more of them left today. Some of the quieter ones who I think would be okay if they weren't scared of her too. Jenny and Karen are going to that new home in the next county and Tracy got into a posh school that takes boarders. Sophie went while I was recovering from the pantry incident.

The numbers are dwindling. With fewer of us here, Thornhill seems bigger, colder. Even less friendly than before, if that's possible.

## May 3, 1982

Today has been mostly okay, at least it was once I found where they had hidden my schoolbag.

In history Mrs. Davies quietly called me to her desk at the front, where she was marking a pile of exercise books. She asked me why my homework had been stuck together with mysterious yellow sludge. She didn't want to say the word *snot*, although as I peered at it across her desk, that was the word that came to my mind. How did they do that? If it was snot, how did they get that much of it? Mrs. Davies was going on about how I should take care of my work and my appearance when she stopped midsentence.

"Mary, are you okay? You look as though you haven't slept for weeks. You look very pasty. You've got even darker rings under your eyes than usual—you look awful . . . " and then I think she realized she sounded a bit rude and she got all flustered. Then someone threw an eraser at the board, and she was distracted.

I took my history book and tried to carefully unstick the pages.

I saw Mrs. Davies glance at me a couple of times during the lesson, as if she was puzzled by something, as if she suspects that something is wrong, but can't put her finger on it. I know she won't take it any further. I am surrounded by adults at school and at Thornhill, but none of them can really see what is happening. They don't want to know. I wonder why that is. What is it that stops an adult from sitting down and really saying, "How are things with you?" or "Is everything okay?" I suspect that they are afraid they might get a truthful answer and then they would have to *do* something, get involved. Or maybe they just can't imagine anything unpleasant or nasty. Maybe they don't *want* to think that something horrid can be happening to people they know.

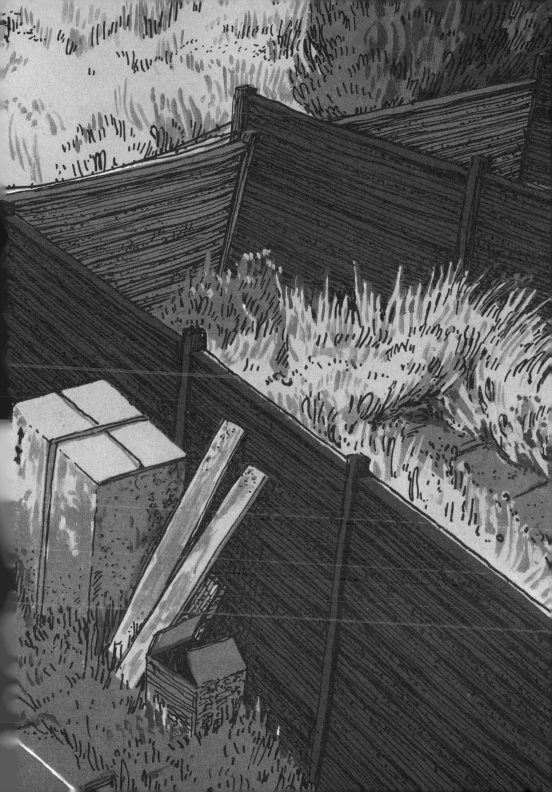

May 4, 1982

I decided this morning that I am going to try to get out a
bit more. Not downstairs, obviously, but out into the
gardens. They are trimmed and mowed and look more
like a park or the gardens of a stately home than the kind
of gardens ordinary people have—those real lived-in
gardens with bikes and trikes and laundry on the line.
The gardens here are lovely, but a bit unfriendly—I half
expect to see a "Do not walk on the grass" sign. But there
isn't one. Not yet anyway.

I have been here for years, but have never spent much
time exploring. Rereading *The Secret Garden* has made me
want to look around. I'm not foolish enough to think that
I will find new friends out here, but I do think being
away from *her* would be good. A bit of head space.

I spent this evening exploring. I crept out while they
were all together watching *Buck Rogers*. The farther away
from the house you go, once you are beyond the gravel
drive where Pete parks his car, the more amazing the
gardens become.

Just past the apple orchard, I found a lovely spot,
surrounded by bushes. It is almost like an outdoor room.
The bushes are trimmed like a wall and there is an

archway cut into the trees with a wooden door in it. In the middle is a statue of a child on a pedestal. It's beautiful. It is lovely and quiet and from inside those green walls I can't see Thornhill—so *they* won't be able to see *me*.

On my way back I bumped into Jane and Pete in the garden. They looked surprised to see me and then went a bit red. Are caregivers allowed to get together? I don't know. It's none of my business, I guess.

I came back in and went to my room. The other girls were busy crashing in and out of each other's rooms, raving about their favorite bands, laughing in an exaggerated, overloud way, or rehearsing lyrics to songs they had recorded from the radio. I walked past doors with posters from *Smash Hits* stuck on them, through wafts of sickly sweet hairspray, and up into my room. None of the others had seen me go in or out. I am invisible again and I am glad.

I have found my own secret garden.

## May 8, 1982

I have had a lovely day. Alone, but quiet and calm. I have spent it outside in the garden, my garden, completely absorbed in making body parts for my new puppets. I prepared my materials last night: the scraping tools for shaping clay and needles for definition and an airtight tin for keeping the bits in, and put them all on a tray. I sneaked down to the kitchen at seven a.m., before everyone else was awake, as Kathleen was just taking off her coat and slipping into her apron. She must have seen me slope out with a yogurt and an apple in my pockets on the way to wedge open the wooden garden door, because when I went back to collect my tray of puppet-making stuff, she had prepared a bacon sandwich wrapped in tin foil and a flask of tea—which she balanced alongside the rest of my stuff with her usual wink.

I can't tell you what a sense of relief I have to be outside, how it feels as though the shadow, the weight of Thornhill, evaporates as I step farther away from its walls. I feel a thrill of freedom to know that I can't be seen or heard by any of them, even though I am within the grounds.

I spent the day in my enclosed garden, hidden from

the house, sitting at the base of the statue with my tray of equipment spread out on the stone step. It wasn't sunny but I didn't feel cold—I was too engrossed in making arms and hands, upper arms, thighs, lower legs, and feet. I am making Colin and Dickon from *The Secret Garden* to keep Mistress Mary company. As I designed all the shapes and measurements, I knew exactly what I was aiming for, exactly what would evolve from my fingertips, as long as I concentrated.

Unwrapping Kathleen's bacon sandwich was a treat. I sat under the statue, munching away, surrounded by teeny body parts, listening to birdsong and the hum of invisible traffic somewhere, and felt as safe and calm and happy as I do when I am up in my room.

I write this back upstairs, the row of arms and legs laid out on my bedside table with the darkness outside my window. I know my night will be disrupted. I know *she* will be here. But I can smell fresh air on my skin and have made and planned and feel more myself somehow.

And I can go back tomorrow.

Kathleen had a flask of tea and a bacon sandwich already wrapped up for me when I went down with my tray of puppet pieces this morning. I like Kathleen. She is kind without any fuss.

The birds were singing and the sun was warm. I felt stronger and happier with each step as I walked across the gravel drive. The sounds of music and the clatter of crockery from the kitchen faded as I walked deeper into the garden, beyond the orchard, behind the toolshed, and under the archway into the enclosed garden. I worked quietly and steadily, gluing strands of embroidery thread to Dickon's head to make his hair. My fingers were cold from the glue, but I could feel the sun on my back and my neck. I thought it was funny that a squirrel came bounding across the grass toward the statue where I was sitting—just as if *I* was Dickon and the animals wanted to be near *me*.

Out there today I felt the embarrassment of their taunts and tricks ease away from me. Out there I couldn't imagine anything sillier than being afraid of a bit of banging on a door.

As I ate my sandwich I thought about how strange the

statue I was sitting under is. It is a young child in a long dress—like an angel, but without any wings. She has her hands cupped, held out in front of her, as if she is asking for something, or waiting for something to be put into them. Begging almost. She is odd, but I like her. I might think of something precious I can give her.

I have been up here in my room since darkness began to fall. I am going to get back to my designs for Dickon's clothes.

# May 10, 1982

I rushed out into the garden after school today. I needed to be away from them all.

I *had* done my homework. I *had*! But when I went to take it out of my bag it was gone.

Mrs. Davies was furious. Clearly any concern she may have almost felt for me a few weeks ago was gone. She asked me to stand up in front of the class and explain where it was. But of course I couldn't. One, because I was in the classroom and she knows, just like all the other teachers, that I can't speak out loud in front of the others; and two, because I just don't know where it is. I remember putting it into my bag this morning. Someone—one of them—must have taken it.

I could hear some of the others in the class sniggering as I stood there. My cheeks were blazing hot. But I didn't cry. I won't ever let them think they have gotten to me. I just stood and thought of Jane Eyre and how she had been humiliated at her school and tried to let Mrs. Davies's accusations that I was "sloppy" and "not taking responsibility for my own actions" wash over me.

No one wanted to pair up with me for the experiment

in science, so I had to do it with Mr. Braithwaite. At lunchtime I sat alone, but still one of them managed to walk past my table and pour orange juice into my lunch.

On the way home from school I kept my head down but I could hear comments like, "Where's your homework, Mary?" and "The mysterious case of the invisible project!" They think they are so funny. But they are not. It isn't funny at all.

So I ran out to the garden as soon as I got home and sat there under the begging girl. I listened to the birdsong and the leaves on the trees, the distant traffic. And I waited until I was calm enough to come back in. I had missed dinner. But when I got up to my room there was a foil-wrapped sandwich and a flask outside my door.

Secret garden? Ha! I can't even get that right. I can't believe I thought I had something, somewhere to myself outside this room.

I didn't notice them at first. I was so wrapped up in what I was doing. It was only when something bounced nearby that I realized someone was throwing tiny hard apples at me from over the wall of hedge. At first they landed close to me. Then one hit the side of my head and another knocked Dickon's head. Then they came thick and fast—bouncing and pattering around me like rain.

Pelted.

Pathetic.

The quiet was over. I tried to gather together my tray of stuff, as if I was packing up anyway, but I was trembling and my face was hot. A flying apple stung the back of my hand. Another caught my neck. I loaded the tray and began to walk, ignoring them as I went under the archway and back toward the house. They called out after me.

"Weirdo!!"

"Can we play dolls too, Mary?"

"Mary talks to her dolls! We heard you, Mary!"

"Freak!"

I ran. The tray shook. Dickon's head tumbled and I

didn't stop to pick it up. When I got back to my room, all I had on my tray was spilled varnish, unused clay, and some tiny apples.

I am so cross that my place has been discovered. I am humiliated, as usual, but mostly I'm sad. Sad that I have left one of my puppets out there. I know it's silly but it feels like I have abandoned a friend. Poor Dickon! Was I talking to him as I made him? I don't know. When I am making my puppets I feel like I am somewhere else. Someone else. And having them around the room with me like this makes me feel less alone. I don't know if that makes me a freak. They called me a freak. I don't care if I am. But I do care that I have left him out there, abandoned, with no one to care for him.

I'll go out early tomorrow and look for him.

They have taken the garden from me. But not my room. I still have up here. I have my books, my puppets, and my words in this diary. I can speak my mind on these pages in a way I can't outside this room. And I can protect it all from them. This is *my* place, and *they* are locked out of it.

Right now I am writing this by flashlight in bed.
It is two a.m.
And I can hear her footsteps climb the stairs.

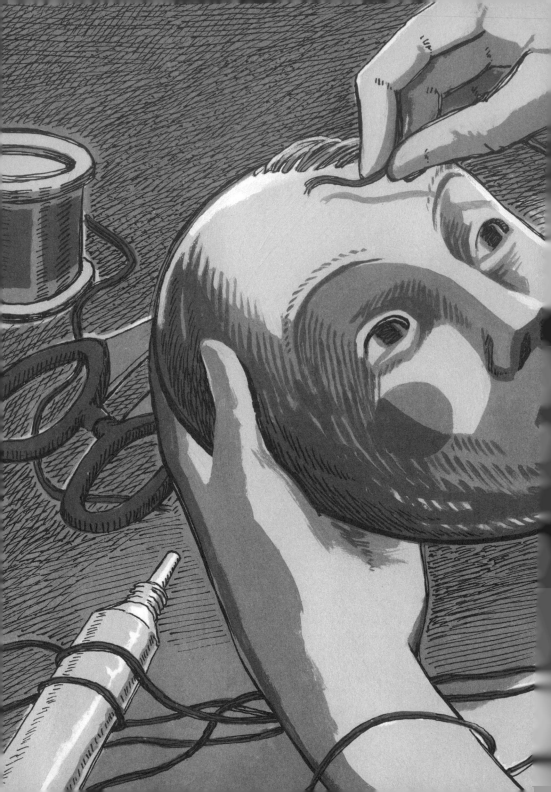

June 3, 1982

There are only six of us left. *She* still has a core group of
followers. They move around the house like a pack of
wolves. It is the five of them and me.

I thought that she would lose some of her power as her
group of supporters dwindled, but the opposite seems to
have happened. It is as if her nastiness has become
concentrated.

There aren't so many practical problems to deal with
during the day. The last three days at school have been
almost normal. I guess she doesn't have so many
followers to do her bidding and she is too sneaky to
be caught.

But every night she is there on the other side of
the door.

## June 4, 1982

This evening I went down to the kitchen to ask Kathleen for some flour. I couldn't find her at first, but the smell of cigarette smoke soon led me to the back door.

Everyone likes hanging out there on warm evenings. They sit on the steps under the brick porch, scraping their names into the brickwork as they puff on cigarettes or whisper about boys. For a hundred years, every Thornhill girl has scratched her name into the brickwork, along with her best friend's name, hundreds of pairs of names scraped into the red brick. All the other girls I have known at Thornhill are on that porch. Only my name is missing.

But tonight it was Kathleen out on the back steps. She was chatting in the twilight with Jane. Both of them had cigarettes and were swigging from mugs. Kathleen's cooking sherry was balanced on the step between them.

They didn't hear me—was it the noise of the washing machine or the fact that I have become an expert at creeping around? Anyway. I wish they *had* heard me instead of me hearing them.

"It isn't right, Jane. You just have to look at her to know she isn't sleeping. She barely eats anything. None of them talk to her. She looks more sickly than ever."

"I know. But, honestly, it's her own fault, if you ask me, Kathleen. It's one thing to have this selective mutism thing—if it really is a thing and she isn't just choosing not to speak—that makes her odd in the first place, but then she spends all her time on her own making those damn dolls. It *is* a bit creepy. She doesn't even try to fit in."

"Just because she is a bit different doesn't mean they should pick on her."

"A bit different! Come on, Kathleen, she's weird. You say they are picking on her, but we don't have any proof. She doesn't ever say anything. She has never made a complaint. How can we help her if she doesn't help herself? She just tiptoes about with that tight, pinched, sour face of hers. She never smiles. No wonder no family wants her . . . If her speech thing isn't problem enough, she is also the least likable girl we have ever had here . . ."

I didn't wait for Kathleen's reply. As I left the kitchen, I heard them chuckling and the chink of china as more sherry sloshed into their mugs.

My chest aches. I liked Jane. I trusted her. I thought she was kind. I thought she understood.

I suppose I should be grateful to Kathleen for trying.

When I got back up here, I stood at my window watching the houses opposite, the regular people with regular lives, trying to work out if what Jane had said was true. Is it all my fault? Have I brought it on myself? Am I unlikable? As I turned it all over in my mind, I watched the lights go on. Families washed up and watered their gardens. They tucked their children into bed and drew their curtains. The house lights cast a golden glow of warmth.

It is tough to be without a family. But to be without a friend too? Is that *really* my fault? Even the caregiver who is paid to care doesn't care, it seems.

I won't let anything any of them says or does make me cry. Ever. But I am aching inside. Maybe this is what heartache feels like.

# Thornhill plans stall again

**ANGER:** Locals and developers angry council's lack of ...ion.

...sion about a development that will provide not only much-needed new homes, but also space for local clubs to meet, as well as a business space."

A spokesperson from the Future Vision Construction Company voiced his frustration that plans to develop the Thornhill site have stalled again.

"We have put forward strong revised plans for this site to become a new community hub at the heart of Midchester. We have taken on board all of the council's previous concerns, but still it seems ...nnot progress. We

Chief local planning officer, Steve Chappell, rebuffed the criticism "For better or worse th... is an important local a... We must think carefu... about the developme... such a sensitive ... our town's recer... We cannot rush ... velopment u... convinced th... historical ... fully Midcheste... fully inte...

not under-
...all is

CRYI
Loca
Sh

## SAD HISTORY

Thornhill Institute was established in the 1830s as an orphanage for girls. It was sold for development in 1982 when the home closed. But after the tragic death of one of the last residents, Mary Baines, the decision was taken to suspend the development until after the inquest into her death. The damning report, by Lord Dudley Grenville of Kingsbury, into Childcare Services led to further investigations and a revision of government legislation.

To this day the council has been unable to decide how to develop the site.

Tragic death : Mary Baines

crying shame that the Thornhill site had been left to decline. "Thirty years that place has stood empty when local people are desperate for affordable housing. The council should be ashamed to have let that old house become such a dangerous, dilapidated old ruin. It is like a beacon of sadness in the heart of our local community."

...
in
...tory.
a de-
we are
...ornhill's
...bution to
...be thought-
...d."

## SHAME

...dent Dorothy said it was a

By Megan Stone

June 16, 1982

Men with clipboards were here today.

As there are only four of us left and only a few rooms on the second floor are occupied, the rooms on the third and fourth floors have been boarded up, so there is hardly anyone between me up here and the staff on the first floor. Tomorrow workmen will be boarding up the empty first-floor bedrooms.

Thornhill is becoming quieter without the chatter of the other girls here but noisier in other ways. It's echoey. Footsteps along the corridors seem louder. Doors closing can sound startlingly noisy. Even the conversation between the clipboard men sounds like a rumble from the floor below. Kathleen doesn't have much to do and spends most of her time with a cigarette and a magazine. Jane seems to be spending most of her time in Pete's room. It's as if the rules don't matter now that there are only a few of us left.

Today my laces were missing from my shoes. I wore them anyway and now have blisters.

## June 23, 1982

I was halfway down the third-floor stairs when I heard the noise. Kathleen and Jane coming from the back of the house, their voices raised. I have never heard Kathleen cross. I've heard Jane's shrill shouty voice when the other girls goofed around too much—but not Kathleen. I stopped where I was on the stairs and they came to a halt on the first floor somewhere beneath me. I couldn't see them, but I could hear everything.

"It's just not down to me, Kathleen! It isn't my responsibility. The social workers, the local authority, it's their call. It's nothing to do with me!"

Kathleen sounded really angry.

"That's just lame, Jane! I never thought I'd hear that attitude from you. You know these girls. You've worked with them for years. Even if you don't have proof you must still suspect what is going on. How can they possibly rehome them together? What will happen to Mary? Don't you care?"

"Kathleen—it's not my job! They wouldn't take any notice of me anyway. It's about money, resources—they aren't going to care that those two girls don't get along. The decisions are made way up the line."

"But I am not talking about it as your job. I am

265

talking about you saying something as a human being who cares about those girls. You're her caregiver, for heaven's sake! Say something. Stand up for her! Make a fuss! Who else can speak on her behalf?"

"You're out of line, Kathleen. You're talking about something you know nothing about!" Jane was really shouting now.

"It's not out of line to care about that girl. If Mary goes to Sunny Rise with that little witch you know she will be miserable!"

"That's enough, Kathleen! You shouldn't speak about any of our girls like that no matter what you think they've done. I've had enough of this conversation."

Jane stomped into view, straight across the hall and out of the front door, slamming it behind her.

"Listen to me!" shouted Kathleen. "Why won't you listen to me?"

The noise echoed off the walls. And then it went quiet. Kathleen's footsteps slowly returned to the back of the house and all was still.

And then I saw it.

The door to *her* room was ajar. I watched it slowly close and heard it click shut.

*She* had been listening too.

Jane came up to my room today. It is almost four months since she was up here last. She started off with all that friendly stuff like before but now that I know it is just a pretense, I kept my back to her and stared out of the window, watching the birds in the top branches of the tree outside.

I won't forgive her for saying, for even thinking, those things about me. Ever.

She said we needed to talk. She asked me if I would sit down with her. I ignored her. There was a long and awkward silence and then she said she had to tell me about the changes here at Thornhill. They were:

1. Tomorrow Rachael and Hannah will be rehomed.

2. Then it will just be me and *her* as residents of Thornhill. Jane and Pete will stay here as our caregivers until we have been rehomed.

3. We are both on the waiting list for Sunny Rise but we have to wait for places to become available. There are twins there who are in the last stages of the adoption process, so two spaces will be free soon. It may be a

month, it may be two, but Jane thinks we will be able to move on by the start of the new school term in September. Obviously (she said) the situation isn't ideal and she knows I would prefer it if I could be rehomed with someone else, but she has discussed it with the social workers and the council and this is all they can offer us at the moment.

4. Kathleen will be leaving next week.

5. The kitchen and dining hall will be closed off but a microwave and a fridge have been put in the TV room for us to use. We should otherwise stick to our rooms, the TV room, the bathrooms and grounds. Work will not begin until we have moved out, but in the meantime there may be surveyors, builders, and council officials around the place.

6. Those of us who are left must all try and get along.

So this is it. Confirmation of all I had been dreading.
I don't want to be left here with *her*.
I don't want Kathleen to leave.
I don't want to leave my room.

Are they *really* going to rehome *her* and me at Sunny Rise? Together?

Can they not see what they are doing? Are they deliberately cruel or do they just not care? Or does it amount to the same thing?

June 25, 1982

I have written Kathleen a note. It says:

*Kathleen,*
    *I heard what you said to Jane the other day.*
*Thank you for trying.*
    *Please don't go.*
    *Don't leave Thornhill.*
    *Can't you ask them to let you stay on until we all leave?*
*I hate life here and it will be even worse if you are gone.*
*You are my only friend and I can't bear to be here without you.*

*Mary*

I have left it in the pocket of her apron, hanging on the back of the kitchen door.

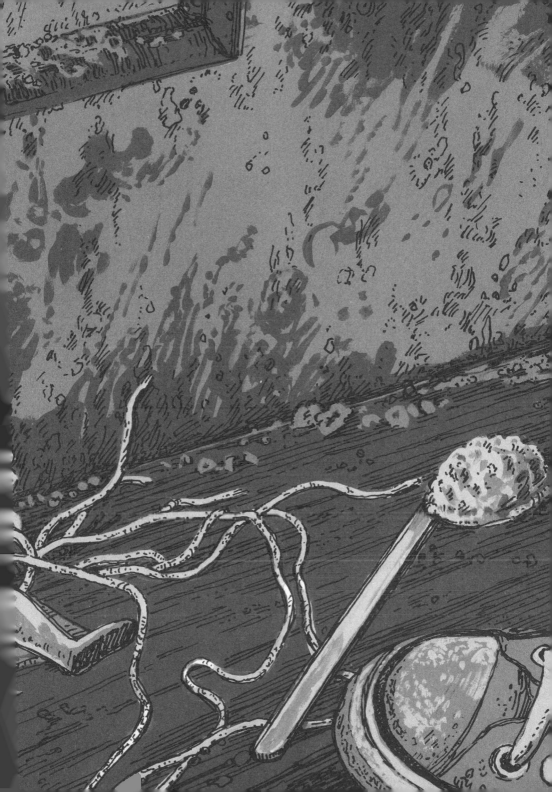

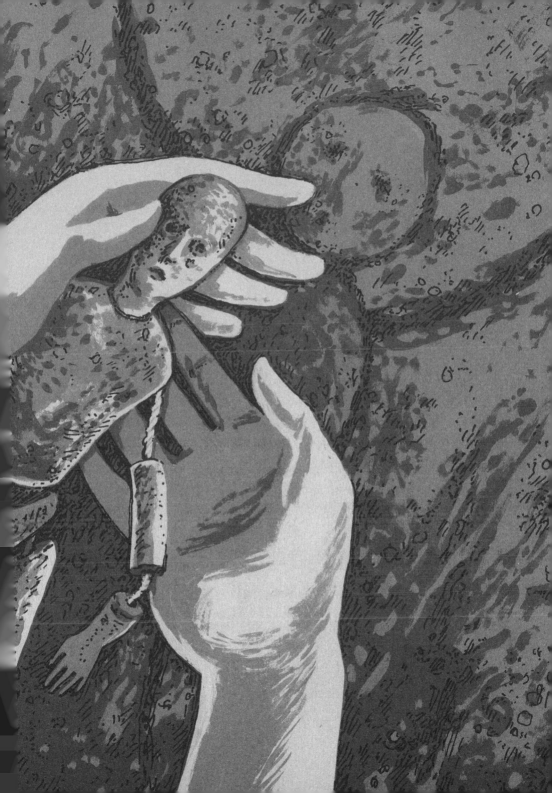

When I got home from school today a card was under my door. It had a picture of a fluffy chick on the front. Inside it said:

*Dear Mary,*

*Thank you for your note. I am sorry to be leaving you and Thornhill. I have worked here for fifteen years and it will be a big change for me—just as it will be for you too. My husband, Frank, has retired and he has booked us on a cruise to celebrate. So even if I wanted to stay I would still be away for a few weeks. I'll send you a postcard. When we get back we are moving away to the coast. Maybe when you are older you can come and visit us there?*

*I will come and say goodbye before I go.*

*Kathleen x*

I am so sad. Everything is slipping away.

## July 2, 1982

Kathleen went yesterday. She came to my room to say goodbye. It is the first time she has been in here. She said something like, "Heavens, Mary! Have you got enough of those puppets?" and looked around with her mouth open. "You must have, what, forty? Fifty? Nice how you have them displayed, though. And your room. Nice and orderly, that's what I like to see." Then she said, "Looks like I can be useful then." And she began to empty out the contents of a shopping bag onto my bed.

It was amazing. There was flour and bowls for mixing papier-mâché paste. She had packs and packs of white modeling clay. Some blocks of balsa wood and some small carving tools. There was wire. String. Hooks. So many things I could use to make puppets with. I didn't know what to say. She had brought me a present to say goodbye. None of it looked pretty, but each thing she unpacked was perfect. She had thought about every item.

I began to cry.

I never cry. I promised myself I would never let them see me cry.

But it isn't their horribleness that made the tears come. It was kindness. Kathleen's lovely kindness.

And then she was hugging me. A real hug. I wrapped my arms around her and sobbed into her apron. She smelled of cigarettes and laundry detergent and that made me cry more. She was talking to me but I was crying so much I couldn't hear it all. She called me a funny little chick and told me I had to stand up for myself and that nothing bad lasts forever. She said that she would write to me with her new address. And then she was gone.

And now that I have started crying I can't stop.

*She* was up here in the night. She stood outside my door listening to my crying. She didn't make a sound. But I saw her shadow beneath the door. Quiet and waiting.

# July 10, 1982

The doctor came today. I heard him ring the bell and explain to Jane that he had come to see me. Someone had raised concerns about my health and well-being, and he would like to see me alone.

He was very polite. He asked to come in, and wouldn't sit down until I nodded that it was okay. He had a soft accent, kind eyes, and tufty gray hair. He chatted about the puppets, and he asked who they were. Some he guessed at—Dr. Jekyll and Mr. Hyde, Jane Eyre and Mr. Rochester with little Giselle and Pilot the dog—some he couldn't. He asked about the books I liked reading. He spied *The Secret Garden* and said how he enjoyed reading it to his daughter years ago. I showed him my Mistress Mary puppet. He chuckled when he saw it and said I had captured her just right. He had a slight whistle in his voice. He propped her up carefully on the pillow and balanced her head to watch us in the room.

He was nice.

He asked me if I was well. He said that a friend of mine had dropped by his office and asked him to stop in and check I was okay. He said that to be well everybody had to look after his or her body—to eat well and sleep well. He also said that to be healthy we had to look after our heads too, and that if there was anything worrying me or bothering me I should tell someone. He asked if there was anything I wanted to tell him.

I wanted to speak.

I wanted to blurt out that I was scared of *her*, that I can't sleep because I am so scared now that it is just her and me.

I wanted to say how I am afraid to be in Thornhill.

I wanted to tell him that even when they close Thornhill, they are planning to put us in the same home, so it will never, ever stop.

I wanted to tell him that although I am afraid to be here with her, I don't want to leave. Thornhill is my home.

But I couldn't.

I couldn't say a word.

What would it sound like to someone else? If I were to say, "She isn't very kind to me and bangs on my door at night." She doesn't hit me, or touch me. I don't have bruises. In fact, for the last few nights she hasn't even touched the door. She just stands silently outside.

I would sound stupid and childish.

He wouldn't believe me.

I couldn't tell.

I can't tell.

I can't find the words.

I looked back at that kind old doctor and whispered that I was fine. That I had just got out of the habit of sleeping.

He made a tight smile, but his eyes looked as if he didn't believe me.

He took a little notebook out of his jacket pocket and slid a piece of paper out from inside. It was my note to Kathleen.

"Mary, your friend gave me this note. This note looks as though was written by someone who is very unhappy. Are you sure, Mary, that there is nothing you want to tell me?"

I shook my head.

He sighed and wrote his name and his number on a piece of paper. He said that I could call him anytime or stop into his office to see him. He said that he would always make time to see me if I wanted to talk. He left the piece of paper on my desk and said that I was clearly a very gifted sculptor and how lovely it had been to meet me.

I leaned over the top banister and listened to him

318

speak to Jane before he left. I couldn't hear it all, but I heard him say "deeply concerned about her well-being" and that "selective mutism is very isolating," that he "will report to a social worker" and that he "questioned the care culture at Thornhill." Jane didn't look too happy as she showed him out.

I have thought about his visit a lot this evening. I wonder what he would have said if I had told him the truth. I feel silly for having been too scared to tell him.

But mostly I think his visit was good for two reasons: firstly, he said a friend had called in at his office about me so, even though she has gone, I know that Kathleen is still thinking about me; and secondly, I have Dr. Creane's number. I'll probably never use it, but it is good to know that I have someone to turn to.

With Kathleen gone we don't eat together, we just go down to take food from the fridge ourselves. I haven't had anything hot for ages.

*She* stays downstairs all the time—usually in the TV room, often with Jane and Pete. Although they are "caregivers," paid to be here with us, Jane and Pete seem to not bother with anything anymore. It is as if all the rules have been suspended. They are supposed to supervise us in turn, but instead they hang around all day together—smooching, watching TV, or shut away in Pete's room.

There is something about this that is worse. They seem to be treating *her* as a friend. Sometimes I hear the three of them laughing together. Chatting. Joking. I've even seen them offering her cigarettes.

I stand listening, watching them from the top of my stairs, peering over the banister to see where they are and what they are doing. I wait to see if the coast is clear for me to go downstairs without bumping into any of them. If they are all up late, or the door to the TV room is open, it means I wait until everyone is in bed.

The mornings are best. I prefer to go down at

five a.m. when it is just light and the birds are singing, and collect enough food for breakfast and dinner, and then sit at my window making puppets until it is time for school. I can go for days without seeing any of them face-to-face, and I don't think I am missed.

Each time I go down, I feel the hairs on my neck stand on end. I creep about, my hands clammy and cold with the prospect of having to face her.

I keep hoping that Kathleen will write. I haven't heard from her yet. Instead I am trying to make a whole family at the same time, molding their heads in turn, building the kind of family I'd love to take me. They are round and freckly and I imagine them to be kind and noisy—a bustling, jokey, jolly, noisy family that wouldn't mind my quietness.

*She* was up here again last night. She stood silently outside the door. I could see her shadow interrupting the sliver of light on the landing. You would think that with her silence instead of the thumping, I would just sleep; rest. Ignore the fact that she is there. And I want to sleep. I am so, so tired. But I can't. I lie awake, waiting for her. I lie as still as I can while she stands there, trying to see if I can hear her breathing on the other side of the door.

Waiting to see what she will do. I know that the key in my door keeps me safe, but my nerves tingle. I hold my breath and try not to breathe. And eventually she slinks away.

## July 15, 1982

Last night was different.

Last night she came up and stood there for the longest time. And then I heard her moving something across the paint on the other side of the door. It wasn't a scratch—more of a scraping sound. And then she left.

When I got up this morning I opened the door.

At first I couldn't see anything. There was nothing there. But I was so sure I had heard something. I ran my hands over the surface of the paint. I felt it before I saw it. It was the letter "F" etched into the gloss—not enough to chip it away, but enough to leave a gray scratch that you could only see if the light was just right. How strange. Why would she make that effort to scratch just one letter?

## July 16, 1982

The same thing happened again last night—only this
morning there was the letter "R" scratched after the "F."

Why?

What is she doing?

What does it mean?


I spent the day working on my new family. My favorite
of the set is the sister. I have given her a little black bob
that scoops out at the bottom, and dark eyes that slant up
at the edges. And freckles. I think I will make her a neck
scarf and jeans. She is pretty and I imagine her happily
chatting away to me as I work on her. I have made her the
opposite of me.

July 17, 1982

This morning it was the letter "I."

She has scratched "FRI."

## July 18, 1982

"FRIE." Each night a little more. I lie awake and wait for the scritch-scratch against my door. What is she writing?

I have stitched a little spotted neck scarf for the sister of my puppet family. It covers where her head will join her body. I think it will look good.

July 19, 1982

Last night she added an "N." I can only think that she is
going to spell out "friend." What else could it be?

## July 20, 1982

I was right. When I got up this morning it was there.
The "D." She has written "friend" on my door. Does she
want to be my friend?

I have fallen for it before. I have believed her
words—and she has made me feel little and foolish.
She has tricked me. Hurt me. Haunted me.

July 21, 1982

I slept last night. I slept the whole night! She didn't come up. There was nothing more on my door.

Is it over?

July 22, 1982

Again, last night. Nothing. No sound. No visit.

Two nights' sleep. Two nights of delicious, deep, uninterrupted sleep.

I think she has stopped.

I have decided to write her a note. All day I wondered about what it should say. In the end I wrote

"FRIEND?"

I am so confused. What happened last night has left me questioning all the things I thought I knew.

I had the note. I wanted to slide it under her door so that it would be there when she woke up in the morning.

I know I am used to creeping about this house on my own, but I wanted to know what it feels like, tiptoeing about in this dark and almost empty house at night, like she does. I wanted to know what it is she feels when she climbs up to my room and stands outside my door. I wanted to understand why she does it.

I waited until two a.m. It was pitch-dark. Inky black. I felt completely awake—tingling with excitement. It was a strange feeling, as if I was the only person in the world, and no one could stop me or see me. It was as if Thornhill belonged to me. I felt powerful.

The house itself felt different. So, so silent. Moonlight shone onto the stairwell as I tiptoed to the floor below.

But as I got near her door I heard another sound. At first I couldn't work out what it was. It was a muffled gasping sound. I stood with my ear to her door, holding my breath. It was crying. Sobbing, in fact. It was such a lonely sound.

I stood, listening. At first I felt a rush of triumph. Now who's the unhappy one! But then I realized what that meant. And I felt ashamed. Ashamed that I could feel pleased that someone was crying in the night with such despair.

There I was, standing outside her door in the dark, listening to her crying, just as *she* had listened to *me*.

I slid the note under her door and crept away. But she must have heard me, or seen the note, because as I reached the second landing and looked back, there she was, her door open, standing there looking . . . awful. Her eyes were puffy and red and swollen with tears. Her hair was disheveled and tangled. She stood in her doorway, crying, leaning against the doorframe, my note crushed tight in her fist. I couldn't recognize her as that confident, rosy-cheeked, bright-eyed beauty that they all had followed with such adoration. She stood there, gazing up at me, tears rolling down her face as her shoulders shook with sobs. She looked small and desperate and helpless.

I looked down and we held each other's gaze. But I couldn't do it. I couldn't go to her. I wouldn't comfort her. I turned and just kept walking as if I had seen nothing, as if I was unaware of her suffering. As I reached the fire door up to my staircase her door clicked shut.

But now that I write this in the comfort of my room, the morning sun streaming through the windows and the birds singing outside, I am haunted by the sight of her and I can't get that sound out of my head.

How can that sad, forlorn-looking girl be the same monster who has tormented me?

What's happened? I don't understand! Yesterday I didn't see her all day. I spent the day up here. I felt sad, uneasy. Confused.

But as always I got absorbed in the making of this new puppet. I stitched a costume; tiny, tiny stitches as I listened to the squeals, laughing, and crying of the children in the nearby houses as they played in the heat. It was too hot. My needle kept slipping in my sweaty fingers. It was a relief as the sun went down and the evening came. I went to bed with my window open and without blankets.

And I slept. But then, at some point, she was there.

At first a scraping, scratching sound and I thought she must be scratching more letters. But then—as before— she started banging on my door.

It began as the usual

Thump.
Thump.
Thump.

But then, it became worse, as I had never heard it before. It was a pounding, a slapping, slamming, kicking, like she was hurling herself at the door, which shook and juddered as if the wood and hinges could barely hold her back.

My head was tight with fear, but this—this was so, so extraordinary I found myself huddled in the corner of my bed, hugging my knees, watching the door, amazed, waiting to see what would happen next.

And what happened was even more unexpected. She started crying, shouting, screaming. I couldn't make it out at first because of the banging, but there were the odd words—the usual—"Freak!"—"Weirdo!" etc., but others such as "Friends!" and, I think, once, "Hopeless!" but I can't be sure.

She must have been making a real racket because Jane and Pete came running up the stairs. I heard the drama unfold outside my door. At first they shouted at her, trying to be heard above her own wild cries. Then came their exclamations to each other as they tried to understand what was happening and tried to calm her down. Jane began talking in a very low, slow, quiet voice, gently questioning until the banging and shouting stopped and everything became still. They led her, still quietly sobbing, back downstairs.

I listened as their steps receded and the fire door swished shut behind them. I lay there in the dark, my heart racing, bewildered, my mind running through what had just happened. I waited for Pete or Jane to come back up and check if I was okay. But no one came.

After a while I got up and went to the window and looked out on the houses. A light was on in one of the windows and someone stood looking out at Thornhill. At least, I thought she was looking out at Thornhill, but then I realized it was a woman with a small child in her arms, rocking it back and forth as she looked out at the night. I stood watching as she gently swayed for the longest time before walking slowly back into the room. For a moment or two she was out of sight, but then I saw her draw the blankets over the sleeping child, smooth them into place, and kiss the child's head. The lamp light went out and that window disappeared in the darkness.

I went back to my own bed, calmed. Moments like that must be happening all around the world every second of every day. For most people that's just normal— so everyday that they won't even think about it. I wonder what it would feel like to have someone be like that with me and I thought of Kathleen and the smell of her apron as she hugged me and called me a funny little chick. As I went to sleep, I decided to think about that instead of the bizarre happenings of the night.

When I opened my door at daybreak this morning it was dented, scratched, and splintered. And gouged deeper into the paint was the word "LESS."

Friendless.

Does she mean me?

Or her?

Thornhill has been silent all day. It is as if there is an illness in the house. As if someone is on their deathbed and everyone is tiptoeing carefully around. It is too hot, too oppressive to move. I have wedged open my bedroom door and the fire door to help create a breeze from my open window, but I don't think it makes much difference. The air is so still. I heard Jane on the phone a few times and Pete and Jane whispering in the entrance hall. At one point I thought I heard Dr. Creane, but otherwise it is all still and quiet except for the doors being clicked shut on the ground floor and occasional footsteps. It feels as if the house itself is holding its breath.

And I am sitting here upstairs. Alone. No one has come up to speak to me, to check I am okay. But that's all right. I have been making my next doll, listening to the quiet and wondering what will happen to us all.

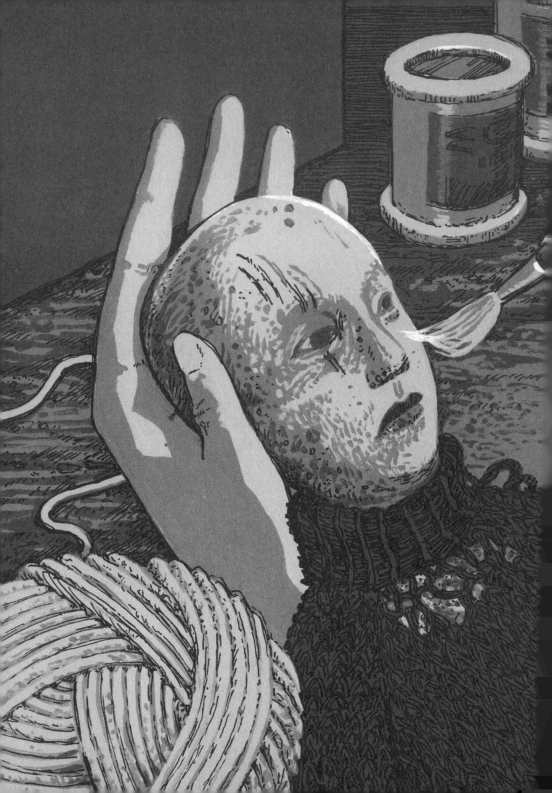

## July 28, 1982

Today's events started when Jane and Pete went out.
Despite everything that has happened this week, they
just walked off down the drive, arms around each other,
laughing, as if they didn't have a care in the world. To
look at them you would never have guessed that they both
work in a house that is becoming eerier and more silent
by the day, supervising two girls that no one wants.

Are they allowed to just leave us like that?

Is that right?

It didn't feel right.

It left just me and her. Alone in Thornhill.

I decided to get out too.

Now that I think back on this morning I realize how
unusual a decision that was. It had never occurred to me
to walk out of Thornhill before—to just walk off down
the drive and out of the gates as Jane and Pete had done.
I decided to go to the library in town . . .

But it never happened.

Instead I am back up in my room. My hand is steady
but my mind is racing.

I think I have done something important.

I think something has shifted.


I packed a bag. Two apples, this diary, the tiny clothes I have been stitching for the puppet family I am making, and some pens. I locked my door behind me as quietly as possible, crept downstairs, and headed for the main door. And there she was.

We were face-to-face.

Her eyes were red. Her face was blotchy.

I stepped to one side.

She stepped in front of me.

I stepped aside again.

She stepped in front of me again. She was crying.

"You can't go, Mary. Stay."

She made to grab hold of the strap of my bag and I swung it away from her, not wanting to be touched by her, not after everything she had done. She lunged at my bag again. I spun it away from her. The contents scattered, skittering across the floor.

I scrabbled around at her feet, picking up the odd pen and my diary. She stood back, completely still, and watched me on my hands and knees. She said, "God, Mary, you're pathetic."

And then it happened. I had a flash of . . . I am not sure . . . Anger? Frustration? Whatever it was bubbled up inside me. The unfairness of it all. How horrid she was. How unkind Jane had been. I was there on my knees at her feet but I knew *she* was *wrong*.

"No!" I said. "No, I am not. I am Mary Baines and I work hard and make puppets and I love books and I do no harm to anyone. I have put up with this house and you without having to be unkind and spiteful and mean. But you . . . *you* have not! It has made you a monster. It is *you* who is pathetic."

My voice shook, trembled, and sounded odd, loud, in the space of the entrance hall. I hadn't picked up everything, but I had my diary—so I ran past her shocked, blotchy face, out of the main door, and around to the back of the house. I hid by the kitchen door, huddled under the porch, catching my breath. Sitting there under all the girls' names scratched into the brickwork, where I had previously felt so alone, I realized I felt something completely different. It was a feeling of . . . power, of triumph.

And it felt good!

Okay—the fumbling around on my hands and knees hadn't been great but I had achieved something. I had spoken. Out loud. And for a fraction of a moment I think she was shocked.

And she had let me go.

It had worked.

Maybe this is the start of something new.

Maybe I can face her.

Maybe I can tell.

Maybe I can speak out.

I sat there under the back porch for most of the morning and into the afternoon. I ate my bruised and dented apples and absent-mindedly read through the pairs of names on the wall.

When I heard Jane and Pete come back in the front of the house, I waited a while and crept back in, just as I have so many times before.

But some of the fear has gone.

I know tomorrow will be different.

Tomorrow I will speak out.

I knew this was going to be my big chance and that I had to get it right.

I made a list of all the things I wanted to say. I wrote down the things that she had done to me, here at Thornhill and at school. I wrote down about Jane, about Sunny Rise. I wanted to make sure that, if words failed me, I would have something I could show them to make them understand.

Dr. Creane's office was full. I had to line up behind harassed mothers with wailing babies and old men with hacking coughs. It was hot and everyone was irritable. I wanted to turn back. But I had gotten this far, this close to getting help.

I wasn't quite sure what to do. I thought that having Dr. Creane's note meant I could see him whenever I wanted.

I rehearsed in my head the words I was going to say and how I was going to say them. I was going to say how miserable I was. That I was lonely. That I was being bullied and that I needed help. I was going to say that I couldn't go to Sunny Rise with *her* and to ask Dr. Creane to speak on my behalf to get me rehomed somewhere else.

We shuffled forward in the line.

I rehearsed it again . . .

I am miserable.

I am being bullied.

I need help.

Don't send me to Sunny Rise with her.

I *had* to get it right. I was almost excited about the idea that I was going to do this. That I *can* speak out and change my life.

The line was so slow. I shuffled forward a few steps more and ran through it all again.

Then it was my turn.

"How can I help you?" asked the receptionist.

I opened my mouth to speak but couldn't. So I fumbled in my bag for Dr. Creane's details.

"Dr. Creane? Do you want an appointment? He is fully booked today. What's it about? Can you see someone else?"

I went red. I shook my head and pointed at the paper. Someone behind me in the line tutted loudly. But I was determined. I *had* to see him. I *had* to speak while I felt strong enough.

The receptionist was saying something like, "You can't just walk in off the street and expect to see

someone without . . ." when there was a click of a door
and Dr. Creane stepped out into the waiting room.

But then I saw *her*.

Her cheeks were red and her eyes were too, as if she
had been crying again. Dr. Creane walked her across the
waiting room toward the door of the office. As he passed
us I could hear him say, "You're a very brave young
lady . . ." She looked up at him and nodded forlornly as a
lone tear rolled down one of her beautiful flushed
cheeks. Then she looked past him and straight at me.

A slight smile played at her lips. Then she was gone.

How can *she* be here too?
Dr. Creane is *my* friend.
He was going to help *me*.

The receptionist was talking at me. People behind me
in the line were grumbling. I left.

And now I write this back at Thornhill in the gardens
under the begging girl statue. The sky is clear and white
with heat, the air is hot and sticky. It is no day to stay

outside, but I don't want to go in. I can't bear the idea of being anywhere near her. She contaminates everything.

Yesterday I thought I could do it. I could speak out. Tell. I could take control.

I knew I couldn't go to my teachers; like Mrs. Davies, they don't want to see what is under their noses. Kathleen would help me, but she is not here. Jane thinks I am weird and is only interested in Pete. Dr. Creane was the only person I could go to, that I could trust, but how can Dr. Creane believe me if he also believes her? How could anyone take me seriously when she is so radiant, so shining? How could he believe that *she* is a monster?

Maybe there is someone else I could go to, but I really can't think who. And the more I think about it, the more my confidence seeps away.

She has done it.

She has taken the one thing that is precious to me and destroyed it.

At first I thought that I had lost my key. But then Jane couldn't find a spare. She saw my panic and she got Pete to call the locksmith. I stood with Jane on the landing as he worked at the lock. He was a round man who was sweating in the heat and puffed as he worked, but seemed jolly. He had a huge grin on his face as he heard the click of the lock and stood back and opened the door with a flourish.

His smile vanished when he saw my room.

Jane gasped.

I heard a loud wailing noise. And then I realized it was me.

My room was trashed.

My books were strewn across the floor, pages torn out. My pens, pencils, schoolbooks had been scattered. My clothes turned out of drawers. It was as though a tornado had ripped through the space.

And my puppets . . .

Each one was missing its head. Their bodies had been flung about the room, torn down from their wall mountings and ceiling hangings and tossed carelessly about the place. Their faces peered up at me from the floor or rested facedown on the carpet. It looked like a bloodless massacre.

*She* had broken everything I care about, invaded my sanctuary and stolen my safety.

The locksmith left quite swiftly. Jane and Pete came up and made sounds of amazement and concern, but I stood rock still until they left me alone.

Now I am sitting here in my room, on the floor, surrounded by chaos and destruction.

And I am shaking. Quaking.

But not with fear.

With anger.

I am burning with it. Hot with rage. I can feel a surge of it within me as if I am swollen with it.

I hate her.

I hate her.

I hate her.

I hate her.

## August 7, 1982

Thornhill is very quiet.

The whole house is holding its breath.

I am staying locked in here. The new key is on my side. No one can get in.

I don't trust myself to see her.

I have such a fury. My anger is like a hot pulse, throbbing, biting, raging.

I am playing through the events of last week. Racing through the scenes. Turning it over and over in my mind.

She must have gotten the key when I swung my bag away from her in the hall.

Is this my punishment for speaking out? For saying what I think?

Jane and Pete have been up, taking it in turns to knock at the door and ask me to let them in, to "chat" about what has happened, to "talk" it through.

I don't want to hear. I put my headphones on and listen to music turned up high. I am certainly not letting them in. I am not letting anyone else in. I don't want anyone to set foot in here ever again.

I can't touch the food they leave for me outside the

door. My throat is too tight to swallow anything other than water.

I have started sorting out my room. I am piling up my papers and taping together my torn schoolbooks. My novels are back on the shelves. My pens and paintbrushes in their pots. I am trying to tidy—to fix it—to put it back in order.

But with my puppets I have another purpose. One by one I am stitching or gluing them back together, mending their clothes and putting them back in their right places. Not all of them can be repaired—some have bits of clay broken or missing—but I am doing my best to put them back together. Except that from each one, I am taking some small part. From each of my beautiful little friends I am taking a hand or a limb or some stuffing or some hair. I have made a pile of heads I will not replace, unhinged arms and legs. A mound of glassy eyes sits on my desk alongside tangled threads of hair. With every snip I make, with each cut, I am thinking of her.

When all the dolls have given me a contribution I replace them carefully, sitting or hanging them gently back where they were, where they can watch the room. Each and every one of them a little bit flawed—except Mistress Mary, that is.

She survived. Mistress Mary is the one that she missed. I found her under the bed, intact. Seems she is stronger than all the rest—just like in the story.

Only in *The Secret Garden* there *is* a happy ending. They become a family, they make one from sad and broken people.

But that isn't going to happen here.

## August 9, 1982

Thump.
Thump.
Thump.


Each time I close my eyes I can see her smile:
that smirk.
I see the heads of my puppets staring up at me from
the floor. Their limbs twisted the wrong way. Their
clothes torn.


Thump.
Thump.
Thump.


I am hungry. But I can't eat.
I can't sleep.


Thump.
Thump.
Thump.

I know that I will show her what she is. What she has done. I am working on my revenge. I snip and cut.

Snip. Snip. Snip.

Thump.
Thump.
Thump.

They want to come in, but I won't let them.
They bang on the door.
They thump, thump, thump.
And my heartbeat pounds in my ears.
I am throbbing with anger.

Thump.
Thump.
Thump.

I've got it!
I know what I have to do.
I have worked out a plan.

# August 11, 1982

I have been awake all night and it is nearly done.

I am dizzy with excitement, hot with anger, sick with hate for her. Sick of her. I am sick of it all.

I have made her. I have taken the remains of my puppets and I have stitched and glued them together to make her—not as *they* see her: not the confident, rosy-cheeked beauty with golden ringlets and blue eyes; but as *I* know her to be: cold, heartless, ugly in thought and mind. She is snot and bile. She is pus and spit and piss. She is a horror and I want her to see what she is.

I have snip, snip, snipped pieces of arms and legs from the bodies of my puppets, and stitched them together to form my life-size monster's face. Her eye sockets made from crushed papier-mâché. arms and tiny hands. The cheeks stitched from tatters of fabric she ripped from my puppets' bodies. I have stuck glassy, beady eyes as warts on her face, and collaged them together as a necklace for my monster. I have stitched tufts of hair into her body, and glued shards of clay and plastic into scales for her skin. I have stuffed her with foam and torn costumes and papier-mâché.

And I have cried. I have cried as I used parts of my old, damaged friends. Cried as I recognized bits of characters I planned and crafted and loved. I had given my time and my care to each of them. They were beautiful. Now these broken pieces are ugly and are building something uglier and I can't stop the tears falling onto my hands as I cut and stitch and glue and scrape.

But now I have made her.

And now I can destroy her.

## August 15, 1982

I am ready. Last night I slid my monster puppet down the stairs and along into the kitchen. It was late and quiet. From Pete and Jane's room I could hear muffled conversation. From hers, sobbing.

This time it was my turn to carry chairs down into the pantry, only I braced them together, back-to-back, between the narrow shelf-lined walls so that I could climb on their backs to reach up high. It took me a few attempts to throw the rope over the pipes that run across the ceiling, but I did it, and then twisted the rope to make a noose. I slipped the noose around my puppet's neck and winched it into place so that it hung down, suspended from its neck. I put away the chairs and stood back to admire my handiwork. She looked magnificent, spinning slowly in the light from the high window, her scales and tufts of hair glinting in the moonlight, her face made from arms and legs and faces of other puppets more terrifying in the half light. I left her there and closed the door behind me.

Then I placed the two letters I had prepared on the main front doormat, one for Pete and one for Jane, so that

442

it would look as if they had dropped there after the postman had delivered them. I took the keys I needed from the office, then I slipped the note I had written to her under her bedroom door. This time she didn't open the door to watch me go back upstairs with those red eyes.

Now I am back up here. Waiting.

And as I wait I am excited. Excited about the plan I have made. I feel in control. I feel powerful.

February 8, 1982

I knew it was too good to last. She is back. Without even looking I knew it. I heard her laughter echoing up the stairwell, the usual thumping on each of the doors in the corridor as she made her way back to her old room. I froze as I heard those sounds. Fear tingled into my neck and down my back as the old feeling seeped into my bones.
I don't believe it.
What will I do now?

April 4, 1982

I can't believe what has happened.
I can't believe I have been so stupid.

She told me yesterday afternoon that they
were going to meet after dark to have a moon
picnic, to celebrate Sophie going to a new foste
family next week, and that she wanted me to
come along. She told me that the old days
when they would have considered going with
me, were gone, and that I am one of them n
I left my room at midnight and crept
to their landing. The wind outside was w
through the chimney pots and made the
adventure seem more dramatic. I was
They were smiling and welcoming, gri
winking at me as we tiptoed down
staircase and past Jane's door.
It was only when we got to th
door that I realized I hadn't even

where the food was coming from.

<u>She</u> was standing by the pantry door.

She put one arm around me and said, "This treat is for us. Just you and me, Mary."

She unlocked the door and we went down the thin flight of steps into the cupboard-like room, lined with tins, packets, jars, and bottles. She pointed to a bottle on the top shelf, up by the tiny window.

"That's Kathleen's cooking sherry." She grinned.

"Come on, give me a leg up!"

She hooked her foot into my interlocked hands and tried to heave herself up a couple of times, but she didn't even get close to the shelf.

"Hang on, Mary. I'll get a chair."

## August 16, 1982

I need to collect my thoughts. To work out what to do.

I want to remember as much of it as I can.

I was up before everyone else. I waited outside the fire door at the bottom of my stairs and watched it all unfold.

Jane emerged from Pete's room and crossed the floor to the doormat where my letters had been joined by a few others from the real postman. They soon did the trick. Jane and Pete were scurrying back and forth, looking for their good shoes, and calling to each other to hurry. They rushed out to Pete's car and were off to an imaginary meeting with Dr. Creane and social workers in the next town. I knew it would be hours before they realized their mistake and were able to get back. By which time it would all be over.

I stood back as I watched her open her bedroom door, my note in her hand. She looked up, but didn't see me. She went back in.

I crept down to the kitchen and hid behind the cabinet unit next to the pantry door.

I waited and watched, remembering her promise of

being a friend in front of everyone in the dining hall.

I watched and waited, thinking of salt in my water, spilled meat down my skirt.

I watched and waited, thinking of all the times I had eaten in that dining hall alone while girls laughed and chatted at other tables around me.

I waited and waited, thinking of the heads of my puppets, smashed and dented, staring up at me from my bedroom floor.

And then I heard the kitchen door click. "Mary?"

It was her.

I heard her walk into the kitchen, stepping around the workers' tools, to get to the pantry door. She was almost beside me. She clicked open the pantry and called down the steps, "Mary? Are you there? I got your note." And then she took a step down, and another . . .

I took my chance, leaping from where I was hiding, and gave her the hugest shove.

The sound of her tumbling down was horrid, but I banged the door shut behind her all the same, jamming the door handle with a chair.

I could hear her shouting, screaming, but I had to follow the plan. I went to each door—the main front door, the back door, the side entrance—and locked them all. It was perfect. She was trapped. She was afraid and now *I* had control.

I sat there with my back against the pantry door. At first I enjoyed her anger as she banged and thumped on the door.

Thump.
Thump.
Thump.

Only this time *she* was on the inside. I felt completely calm as I poured out the kerosene I had taken from the shed onto the floor and began to sweep it under the gap in the door. I poured it little by little, sweeping it under the door, imagining it running around her feet and down the steps.

She screamed more. She shouted and raged, begged me to let her out and to get away from this hideous thing, asking what I was doing. What was this stuff?

Then I sat down again, the matches ready in my hands. I sat quietly and listened as the door bumped and trembled against my back. And I felt good. I enjoyed her fear.

Dear Mary,

Your name is Mary, isn't it? I found your diary. Such sad things have happened to you. You must be lonely. But we are neighbours, and maybe we could be friends too?

Ella

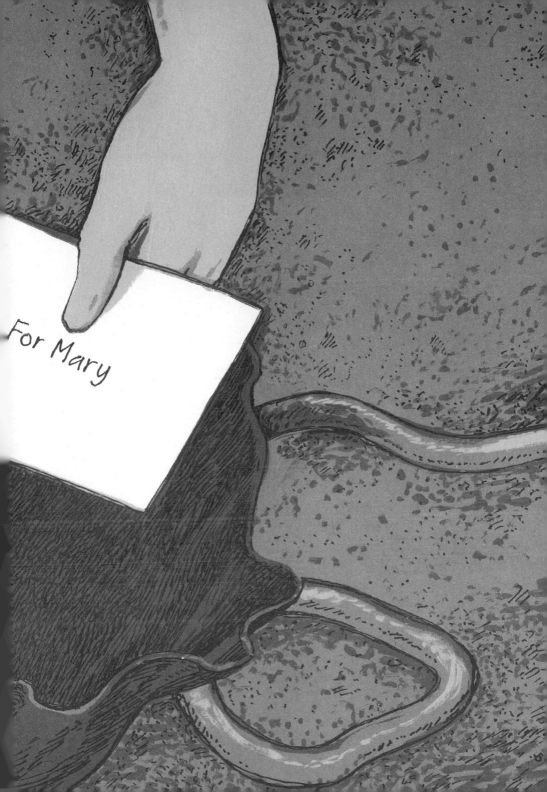

And then she went quiet.

I heard her slide down the door and sit with her back to it. She must have been sitting in a pool of kerosene. Her shouts eased into hiccupping sobs, but mostly she was still. And we both sat there, back-to-back. Her on one side of the door, me on the other.

Then she started to talk.

"Mary, is that . . . thing . . . is that made out of your puppets? Is that what you have made from the pieces I left? Mary, it's hideous and your puppets were so beautiful.

"Mary, I am so, so sorry. I didn't mean to break them. I didn't want to ruin everything. I went in your room and it was so . . . amazing. Your books, your puppets. You didn't need any of us because you had it all there—everything about you is in that room. And I couldn't bear it that you would never let me in . . . I know I have been horrible. I know I have made you miserable. But you were the only one I could never get a reaction from, who wouldn't just follow me blindly. Of all the things I did, we all did to you, you never reacted. It was only once Kathleen left that I heard you crying. And I realized you wouldn't cry because of me. So I stopped, Mary, didn't I? But I still came up to your room at night. I wanted us to be friends. I even wrote it on your door. But you walked away. Like everyone else you turned your back on me. I even asked you to stay and you went. You called me a monster and you are right. I have become a monster so that they will notice me. Listen to me. But no one really hears what I am trying to say. They see this face, Mary. They read my records. I am trying to ask for help and they don't see it. They don't see me.

"We are the same, Mary. We are the voiceless ones. We are invisible. It doesn't have to be like this, Mary. Last night I packed a bag. It's in my room now. I would be away from here if I hadn't gotten your note. I want a new start—not the one they have planned for me, but one where I can start afresh. Mary, you could come—we could leave Thornhill together. We could be friends. Please, Mary. It's this place. It's Thornhill. It made a monster of me years ago and now it is doing the same to you, Mary. Let's get away.

"Please Mary.

"Please."

What she said was so unexpected. I didn't know what to do. I quietly got up and walked away and left her there. I have come up here to think it through.

Could *I* have misunderstood? Maybe she really did want to be friends, to ask me, and didn't know how. I have a sinking feeling that I have made a terrible mistake and just as Jane and Mrs. Davies misunderstood me, *I* have misunderstood *her.* She has been unkind to me, but has she been trying to change and I just couldn't see? I thought of her tear-stained face at the doctor's office, the sound of her sobbing in the night.

Is she right? Is it really this place, this life that made her that way? Am *I* turning into a monster too?

I thought of my anger as I made my ugly puppet. It would be down there now, slowly turning on its noose. One hour ago I was so consumed with a fiery rage, I would have set light to her, to me, to Thornhill. Now the anger has gone, evaporated, and I just feel bewildered. Have I really become so inhuman as to think of destroying another person?

It is not her fault.

It is not my fault.

Somehow it is all wrong.

I went back downstairs, my steps echoing loudly through the empty house.

She was silent on the other side of the pantry door.

My hand shook as I turned the key in the lock.

She was standing there, facing me, as I opened the door. Her face was bruised and her jeans were wet with kerosene.

I smiled at her.

She smiled back.

For a moment I thought we really could be friends. We could leave Thornhill together.

I reached out as if to give her a hug.

But then I noticed that her smile didn't reach her eyes. Her expression was cold. Hard. Her stare dropped to my arms and then back to my face. The smile became a sneer.

"Don't be an idiot, Mary. You didn't really think I would take you with me, did you?"

She shoved past me. Pushing me down those steps. I was tumbling just as she had hours before.

She looked down on me from the top of the stairs.

"Freak!" she shouted, and she was gone.

I lay on the floor, listening as she ran around the ground floor, trying doors. Eventually I heard glass break and all went quiet. She had gone. I was alone.

She had taken my last scrap of hope with her. I lay on the floor in the pantry, unhurt but broken. She had fooled me again. All that anger. All that planning and I hadn't had my revenge—I couldn't even get that right. Am I so desperate for a friend that I would believe anything she said?

I watched the monster puppet spinning slowly on the end of her rope.

It is just me here in Thornhill.
And I know what I have to do.

It took me a while to unhook my monster puppet from her noose. But I did it. I carried her, like a child in my arms, up the pantry steps and out into the main hall, past all the locked and empty bedrooms on the second, third, and fourth floors.

Once I was back up here, I wrapped her in a blanket, and, just as I had seen that mother do in the dark all those nights ago, I stood at my window and rocked my ugly monster back and forth. I wanted to show her some kindness. I sang her a lullaby and then laid her in my bed, tucking the blankets around her so that she was snug, her head resting on my pillow. I covered her with a blanket so she could rest in the warm and the quiet after I had gone.

I straightened everything in my room. I made sure my puppets hung neatly above the bookshelves, my dolls sat up straight between my books. I folded everything away in the drawers. My room is in order.

For the last time I stood and looked out over the treetops and watched the birds fly free. Somewhere out there *she* is free too. Free from Thornhill. Would she ever be free from what it has made her?

And me?

I cannot leave.

I cannot walk away from Thornhill.

I cannot leave my patched and broken puppets. They are my friends and my family. They have been my companions no matter what. They have heard it all and seen everything. They are here and Thornhill has been my home.

So this is my last entry in this diary.

When I have finished this page I will leave it on my windowsill and hope that one day someone will care enough to read it and that one day someone will understand.

I am going to lock this room and hide the key in the secret garden where I have been so happy.

And then?

I will end it where it all began.

I will go back down to the pantry where it all started to change.

I will make sure they can't ever send me away.

And I'll make sure that I stay here, at Thornhill, for as long as I choose.

It is *my* choice and I choose Thornhill.

I will never leave.